To Connie and her great ideas

Copyright © 2021 by Angela Dominguez
Published by Roaring Brook Press
Roaring Brook Press is a division of Holtzbrinck Publishing Holdings Limited Partnership
120 Broadway, New York, NY 10271
mackids.com

Library of Congress Control Number: 2020911296

ISBN 978-1-250-23109-3

Our books may be purchased in bulk for promotional, educational, or business use. Please contact your local bookseller or the Macmillan Corporate and Premium Sales Department at (800) 221-7945 ext. 5442 or by email at MacmillanSpecialMarkets@macmillan.com.

The illustrations in this book were made with watercolor paint, colored pencil drawings on illustration board, and Photoshop.

First edition, 2021
Book design by Aurora Parlagreco
Printed in China by RR Donnelley Asia Printing Solutions Ltd., Dongguan City, Guangdong Province

1 3 5 7 9 10 8 6 4 2

I Love You, Baby Burrito

Angela Dominguez

Roaring Brook Press
New York

¡Hola, bebé!

You're finally here,
mi dulce, my sweet.

This is your home,
tu casa,

where we promise to keep you safe.

And we're
your parents,
tus padres.

We are so pleased to meet you.

This is your delightful **carita**,
which I think looks a little bit like mine.

And these are your precious
manitas

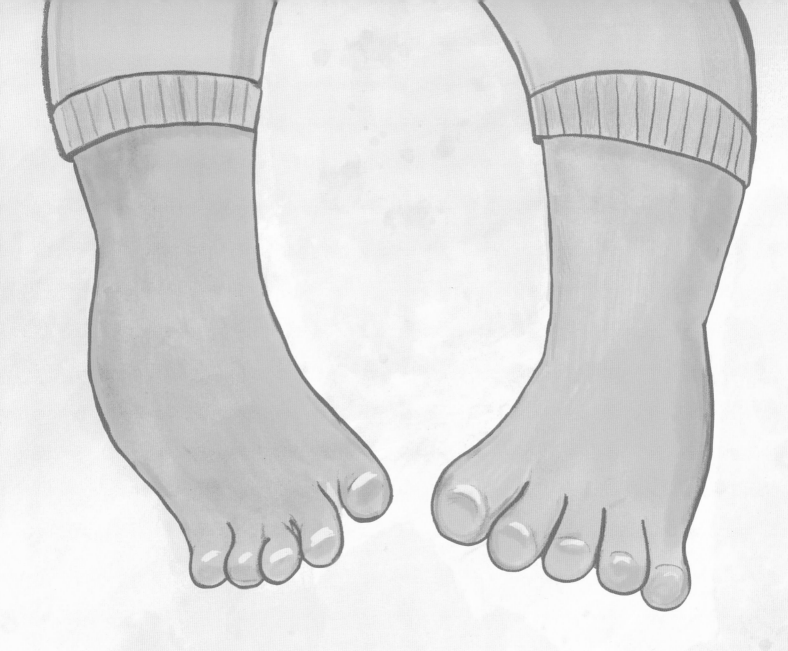

and **deditos**...

that I could gobble up.

Speaking of . . .
Are you hungry?
¿Tienes hambre?

I thought so.

Much better
now that you are
contenta.

And some gentle pats on your back might help, too. Aw, **¡perfecto!**

Well, you've had
a big day.

¡Un gran día!

The first of many.

Now it's time for a **siesta**.

So let's wrap you up,
my precious gift,
mi regalo.

With a cozy, **suave** blanket, I tuck in

each **piernita**,

each **bracito**,

everything except . . .

that **carita**, which, on second thought, might look more like your **papá's**.

Mi hermosa, my beautiful . . .

Did we mention we love you?
We do, ¡muchísimo!

Buenas noches,
mi baby burrito.

Glossary

hola (**oh**-la): hello

bebé (beh-**beh**): baby

mi dulce (mee **dool**-seh): my sweet

tu casa (too **kah**-sah): your house

tus padres (toos **pah**-drehs): your parents

carita (kah-**ree**-tah): little face

manitas (mah-**nee**-tahs): little hands

deditos (deh-**dee**-tohs): little toes

¿Tienes hambre? (**tyeh**-nehs **ahm**-breh): Are you hungry?

contenta (kohn-**tehn**-tah): happy

For Aunty Pat. Thank you. —RY

For Tina, my girl with the broken eggcup —MO

Dial Books for Young Readers
Penguin Young Readers Group
An imprint of Penguin Random House, LLC
375 Hudson Street
New York, NY 10014

First published in Australia 2015 by Scholastic Australia
Published in the United States 2016 by Dial Books for Young Readers
Text copyright © 2015 by Rebecca Young
Illustrations copyright © 2015 by Matt Ottley

Published by Penguin

Printed in China
ISBN 9780735227774

10 9 8 7 6 5 4 3 2 1

Text set in Slimtype Sans

TEACUP

Rebecca Young

Matt Ottley

Dial Books for Young Readers

Once there was a boy who had to leave his home . . . and find another.

In his bag he carried a book, a bottle, and a blanket.

In his teacup he held some earth

from where he used to play.

Some days the sea was kind,

gently

rocking him

to sleep.

Some days the sea was bold,

and the boy held tightly to his teacup.

Some days shone bright

on an endless sea of white.

Other days were so dark

that the boy longed for the stars.

Every day he watched the horizon for a speck that he could follow

until it grew into something glorious.

But there was no sign of land.

As the boy stared at the sky,

an albatross cut across the blue.

The way it dipped

and dived

reminded him of flying kites

back home.

The taste of salt on his lips

reminded him of the sea breeze,

whistling through his favorite tree.

The way the whales called out to one another

reminded him of how his mother

used to call him in for tea.

And the way the clouds slowly swam into view

reminded him of how things

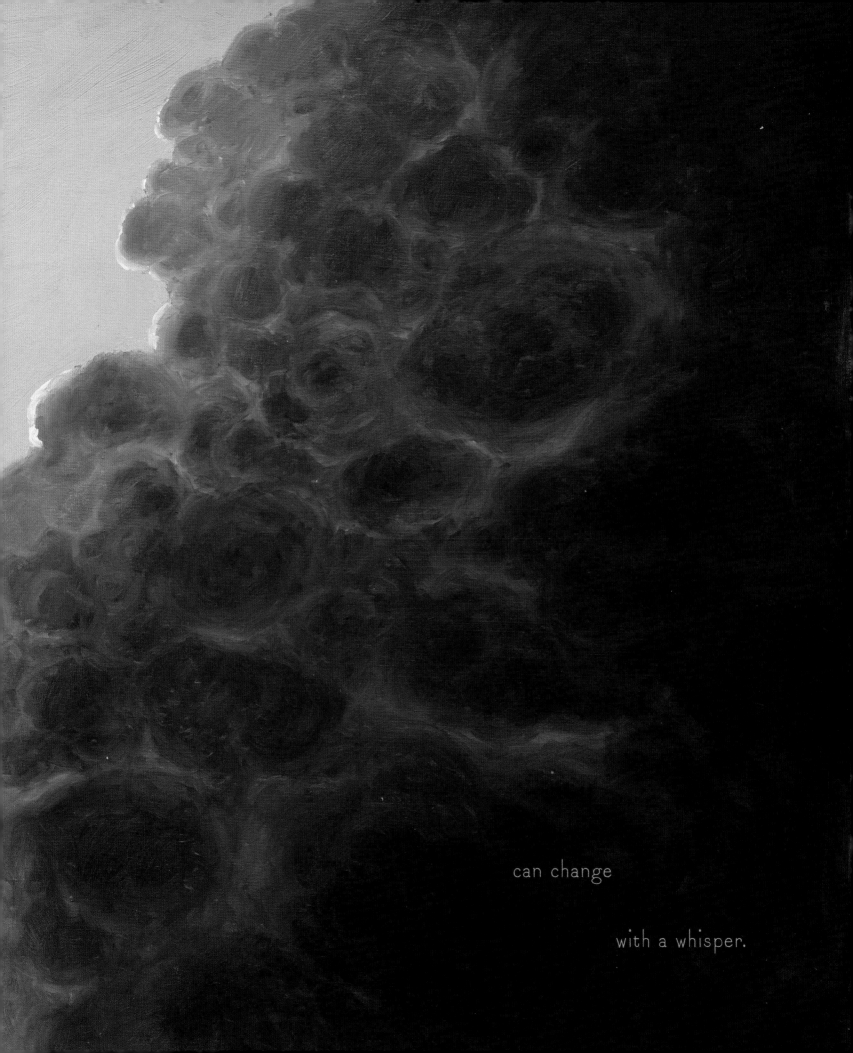

can change

with a whisper.

The boy awoke to something new.

Over trembling seas it grew . . .

and grew . . .

and grew.

The tree gave him shelter and shade,

apples to eat, branches to climb,

and cozy nooks that he knew were

just perfect for daydreaming.

From high . . .

he continued his search for a speck on the horizon.

When he first saw it, it was so very small

that he wasn't certain

he'd seen anything at all.

But before long,

there was a bump.

The boy was happy with what he saw.

There he began to build,

and he waited for a whisper.

Until . . .

the day the girl with the broken eggcup arrived.